THE WORLD OF WORLD MONSTER WRESTLING

ADAPTED BY MAGGIE TESTA

SIMON SPOTLIGHT
An imprint of Simon & Schuster Children's Publishing Division
New York London Toronto Sydney New Delhi
1230 Avenue of the Americas, New York, New York 10020
This Simon Spotlight paperback edition January 2022

For information about special discounts for bulk purchases, please contact Simon & Schuster
Special Sales at 1-866-506-1949 or business@simonandschuster.com.
Manufactured in the United States of America 1121 NGS
2 4 6 8 10 9 7 5 3 1
ISBN 978-1-5344-8250-0

Welcome to the World of **WORLD MONSTER WRESTLING**! We have some exciting matches lined up for you on today's card. First up: reigning Big Belt champion, **KING GORGE**, and the talented up-and-comer **TENTACULAR**! Both monsters are evenly matched when it comes to height, weight, and power, but something tells me that Tentacular just might come out on top.

Who do you think will win between these two heavyweights? You can decide! Act out the match in the wrestling ring using your paper monsters!

Not every match is as glorious as World Monster Wrestling's premiere event. We've got the major leagues and the minor leagues. We've even got the minor, minor leagues. This is fan-favorite **AXEHAMMER** and the very nervous **NERDLE**.

Do you think Nerdle can stand up to Axehammer, or will his wrestling dreams go out the window?
NO, NO! OW!
NERDLE

Remember when we mentioned the minor, minor leagues? Well, this is the minor, minor, minor leagues. Meet **STEVE THE STUPENDOUS**, who has never won a match, and **KLONK**, who just seems to want to get this over with.

GET READY FOR THE MOON BOOM!

STEVE THE STUPENDOUS

Will Steve surprise everyone and win his very first match, or will Klonk knock him out?

THIS LITTLE PIGGY'S COMING HOME!

KLONK

Looks like Steve the Stupendous has got himself a new coach. It's Winnie Coyle, daughter of legendary coach Jimbo Coyle. He coached World Monster Wrestling champion Rayburn Senior. Let's see if Winnie has gotten Steve into shape because he's about to go up against **WHAM BAM RAMARILLA JACKSON**!

Will Ramarilla ram Steve back down to the minor leagues, or will Steve run away with the win?

Steve the Stupendous has managed to get himself a match at World Monster Wrestling's Monday Night Roar. He's going up against **LUCHO LUCHON**. This match is unlike anything we've ever seen before in monster wrestling. It looks like Steve is doing the tango with Lucho.

Can Lucho tango his way out of trouble,
or will Steve's fancy footwork bring him victory?

For his next match, Steve goes head-to-*heads* with **THE TWINS**. The twins might not be big, but they work together to take down their opponents. With two heads against one, will Steve be able to stand up to the pressure?

THE TWINS

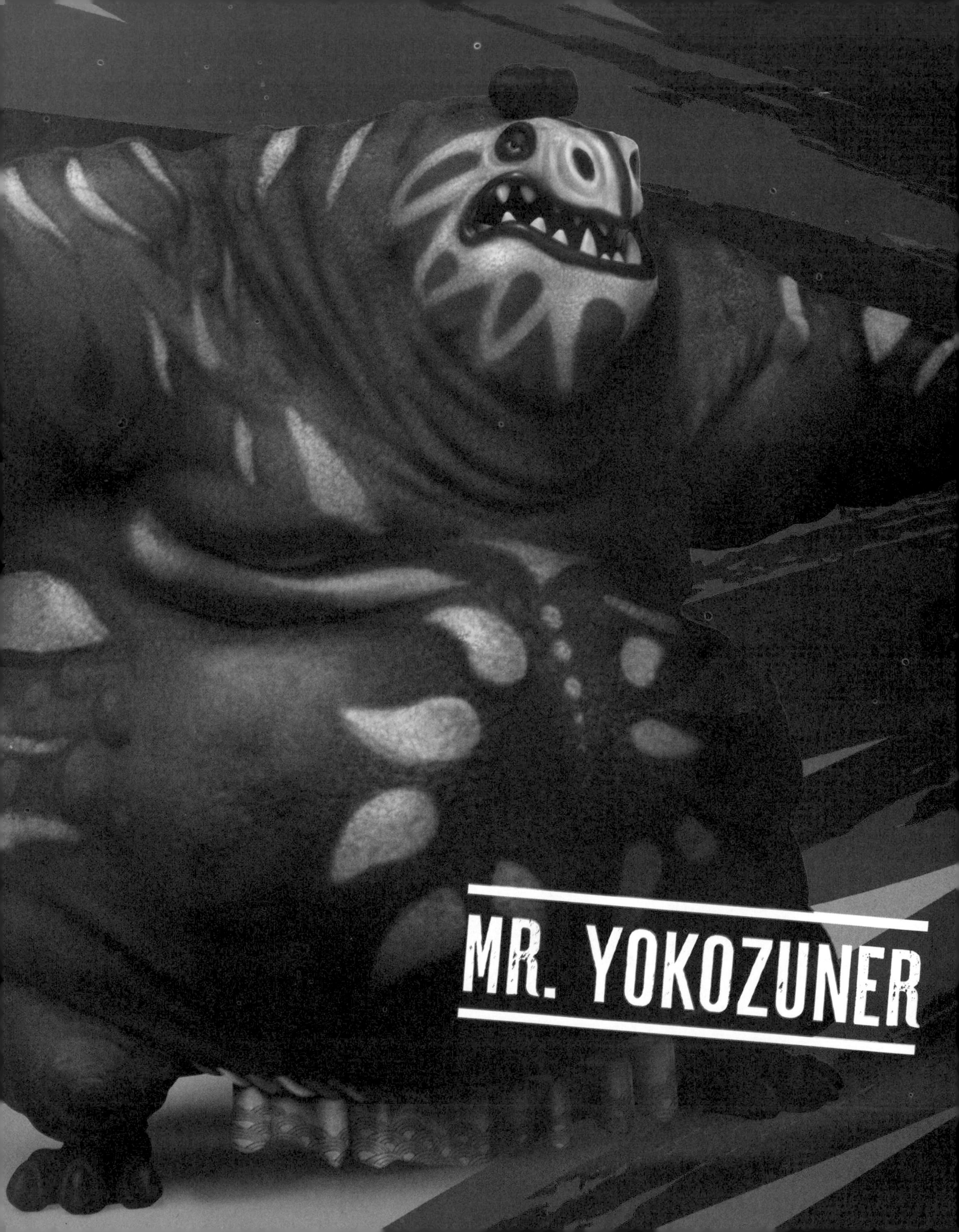

MR. YOKOZUNER

From two small monsters to one giant one, Steve's next opponent is **MR. YOKOZUNER** from the World Monster Wrestling Eastern League. This monster towers at sixty-one feet of pure fury. But lo and behold, Steve the Stupendous isn't letting Mr. Yokozuner's size scare him.

Can Steve dance his way to victory against his fiercest opponent yet, or will Mr. Yokozuner bring the pain?

What's next for Steve, the up-and-coming World Monster Wrestling phenomenon? Looks like he wants to fight his next match back in Stoker. And that's not all. He's not really Steve the Stupendous. He's actually **RAYBURN JUNIOR**, the son of the Greatest of All Time, Rayburn Senior!

Maybe one day he'll even battle that tenacious competitor **TENTACULAR**. Who do you think would win?